Green Kids Act Series

The Gulf Oil Spill Story

Simone Lipscomb

Turtle Island Adventures, Inc.   Asheville, North Carolina

Turtle Island Adventures, Inc.
PO Box 9542
Asheville, North Carolina USA 28815
www.TurtleIslandAdventures.com

The Gulf Oil Spill Story

ISBN 978-1-4507-7614-1

Library of Congress Control Number
2011928884

Layout and cover design by Simone Lipscomb

Be an Earth steward with every choice you make.

To All Green Kids on Mother Earth

With Love

There once was a place where the pelicans played,

In blue-green waters, most every day.

They sat on the beaches or flew in the air,

This place was special, it was quite rare.

The sky was blue, the beaches were white,

The dunes and sea oats were quite a great sight.

Children waded in water and played on the shore,

This beautiful place, many people adored.

Many creatures made the beaches their home,

From the edge of the water, they did not roam.

Ghost crabs dug tunnels and stayed there a lot,

To hide from danger or when it got hot.

In the waters of this ocean so blue,

Spotted eagle rays swam, ate and grew.

They lived on the bottom and fed in the sand;

Hunting for dinner was all they did plan.

Manatees lived in the clear water, too;

They ate plants and slept on the surface of blue.

Many creatures lived in the Gulf of Mexico,

It once was a clean place, they say this is so.

Alongside the sponges, did sea turtles glide;

And jellyfish on strong currents did ride.

The beauty and value of such a great place,

Is sometimes forgotten, is sometimes laid waste.

Now, under the water, far underground,

Are many places where oil can be found.

We pump it and use it to make our cars go,

But it causes problems, this is so.

We drill more and more to find oil and gas;

We use too much and it's not gonna last.

So we hurry and scurry to build more rigs;

We might be considered oil-hungry pigs.

One day in the Gulf, not that long ago,

An accident happened, a big rig did blow.

Eleven men died in the horrible blast;

Then oil gushed up, and it gushed up fast.

Kids waited and watched for the slick to appear;

There was such sadness and so much fear.

What would happen to the water and air?

To the fish, the crabs, the birds? Who would care?

Lots and lots of oil sloshed ashore.

It covered fish, crabs, rays, turtles, and more.

Oil coated the feathers of birds on the beach;

It stuck to everything within its reach.

People came to see it, to see what we'd done;

The oil gushing and gushing was not any fun.

It burned their skin, nose, throat, and eyes;

They wondered if drilling in the ocean was wise.

The pelican's beaches were covered in tar;

It was everywhere they flew, both near and far.

Many got sick and could not fly away;

What a sad mess for so many days.

While beaches were covered in brown oily goo,

No swimming or wading for me or you.

No sand castle building or flying a kite;

"Stay away from the oil!" It is only right.

The fumes burned the gulls as they breathed them in;

Drilling carelessly made nobody win.

Our wildlife friends are treasures for sure;

But look what our greed caused them to endure.

Ghost crabs lay dead near the oozing black tide;

There was nowhere to go, nowhere to hide.

Birds walked among them, eating them up;

The birds then got sick from the horrible yuck.

So the workers came down to the water and beaches;
To clean up the mess, help us learn what it teaches.
No matter how much oil and tar they found,
There was always another ga-zillion pounds.

Some of them worked during hot summer days;
Others worked nights on the beaches and bays.
With shovels and scoopers they picked up the tar,
But we knew for sure the Earth would be scarred.

Some people helped with birds that were sick;

They washed and cleaned them, oh, so quick!

And believe it or not, some birds were saved;

What a gift to the wildlife, these kind people gave.

Now the pelicans gather, those who pulled through;

And we all wonder, "What will they do?

Is it safe to eat fish, is it safe to dive?

Will wildlife still live here, can animals survive?"

Will the Willet find food as she walks on the shore?

Can there be other oil spills? Can there be more?

How can we drive our trucks, buses and cars?

Without oil and gas, can we go that far?

An answer lies waiting, behind the oil rig;

The sun has clean energy and it is so big!

A safe way to make our silly cars move,

That's what we need, we must get in the groove.

The animals are waiting, they want to know;

What will you do to help our Earth grow?

Can you help stop pollution and keep it all clean?

Are you willing to be a kid that is green?

The 'gators are wondering what you will do;
Will you be an Earth steward, will you be true?
Expand your mind and believe in new ways;
For sure, this great planet we all can save!

So next time you're diving under water so clear,

Remember that small or big, all life is dear.

May you find no tar balls, just only big fishes,

That's what we want with our dreams and wishes.

Think of how you, with your parents and friends,

Can help the Earth, can help it mend.

Reuse, recycle, and buy less stuff,

Use less plastic, enough is enough!

Are there things you can do to help the Earth?

Shall we all join together to give it new birth?

Let's love the planet and act really green,

And be kids of action—ahead full steam.

No matter our size or what we can do,

We can all make a difference, this is so true.

Look ahead to the future with love in your heart,

That's the place to begin, the place to start.

Daily Checklist for Kids & Families

_____ Reuse items

_____ Recycle metal, aluminum, paper, glass & plastic

_____ Compost

_____ Turn off water when brushing teeth

_____ Unplug all electronic chargers when not in use

_____ Combine trips, use less gas or diesel

_____ Turn off unnecessary lights

_____ Fix leaking faucets

_____ Grow at least one plant you can use for food

_____ Recycle all used batteries & use rechargeable batteries

_____ Volunteer for an environmental organization

Resources for Kids

EPA—www.epa.gov/kids

Green Kids Act Blog—www.greenkidsact.com

Meet the Greens—www.meetthegreens.org

Kid's Astronomy—www.kidsastronomy.com

Kid's For Saving the Earth—www.kidsforsavingtheearth.org

Kid's Planet—www.kidsplanet.org

National Geographic—www.kids.nationalgeographic.com/kids

National Park Service—www.nps.gov/kidszone

National Wildlife Federation—www.nwf.org/kids

NOAA—www.oceanservice.noaa.gov/kids

PBS Kids—www.pbskids.org

Simone Lipscomb is a writer and photographer. *The Gulf Oil Spill Story* is Simone's fourth book. *Sharks On My Fin Tips*, her first book, is filled with true stories of adventures with nature while scuba diving, cave diving, kayaking, mountain biking and more. *Place of Spirit* is a photography book filled with images of nature from around the world. The final chapter focuses on the Gulf Oil Spill. Simone collaborated with poet, Thomas Rain Crowe, as photographer in *Crack Light*. It contains poems and images from the Southern Appalachia Mountains.

Simone's mission, in creating the Green Kids Act Series of children's books, is to educate and empower kids of all ages to be honorable planetary stewards.

You can learn more about Simone's work at her web site www.TurtleIslandAdventures.com.

The Discovery of DNA

Camilla de la Bédoyère

WORLD ALMANAC® LIBRARY

Please visit our web site at: www.worldalmanaclibrary.com
For a free color catalog describing World Almanac® Library's
list of high-quality books and multimedia programs,
call 1-800-848-2928 (USA) or 1-800-387-3178 (Canada).
World Almanac® Library's fax: (414) 332-3567.

Library of Congress Cataloging-in-Publication Data

De la Bédoyère, Camilla.
  The discovery of DNA/ by Camilla de la Bédoyère.
    p. cm. — (Milestones in modern science)
  Includes bibliographical references and index.
  ISBN 0-8368-5851-4 (lib. bdg.)
  ISBN 0-8368-5858-1 (softcover)
  1. DNA—History—Juvenile literature. I. Title. II. Series.
QP624.D123 2005
572.8'6'09—dc22
              2005040470

This North American edition first published in 2006 by
World Almanac® Library
A Member of the WRC Media Family of Companies
330 West Olive Street, Suite 100
Milwaukee, WI 53212 USA

This edition copyright © 2006 by World Almanac® Library. First published by Evans Brothers Limited. Copyright © 2005 by Evans Brothers Limited, 2A Portman Mansions, Chiltern Street, London W1U 6NR, United Kingdom. This U.S. edition published under license from Evans Brothers Limited.

Evans Brothers Consultant: Dr. Anne Whitehead
Evans Brothers Editor: Sonya Newland
Evans Brothers Designer: D. R. Ink, info@d-r-ink.com
Evans Brothers Picture researcher: Julia Bird

World Almanac® Library editor: Carol Ryback
World Almanac® Library cover design and art direction: Tammy West

Photo credits: (t) top, (b) bottom, (r) right, (l) left
Science Photo Library: /A. Barrington Brown cover, 5, 22(t); /Alfred Pasieka cover, 4(t), 20(t), 25(b), 26(l), 30; /Novosti 4(b); /Bluestone 6(t); /J.W. Shuler 6(b); /Tony Camacho 7; /A. Crump, TDR, WHO 8; /Damien Lovegrove 9(t); /Dr Gopal Murti 10(t), 27(b); /George Bernard 10(b); /Renee Lynn 11; /12, 13(b), 16, 19(b), 20(b), 22(b), 26(r); /Sinclair Stammers, prepared by Andy Cowap 13(t); /James King-Holmes 14; /J. De Mey, ISM 15(b); /T. H. Foto Verbung 18(t); /Eye of Science 18(b); /John Bavosi 24; /Ian Boddy 27(t); /Peter Menzel 28; /Andy Harmer 29(t); /ISM 31(b); /Astrid & Hanns-Frieder Michler 32(t); /David Parker 32(b); /J. C. Revy 33(b); / Hans-Ulrich Osterwalder 34(t); /Tom Myers 35(t); /Chris Knapton 35(b); /James King-Holmes 36(t);/P. H. Plailly/Eurelios 36(b); /Mark Clarke 37; /Simon Fraser/RVI, Newcastle-Upon-Tyne 38; /James King-Holmes 39; /Laguna Design 40; /BSIP, Laurent 41; /Lawrence Lawry 42(t); /Roger Harris 44. Science Society & Picture Library: /Science Museum 3, 23(b), 29(b), 42(b). CORBIS: /© Chris Collins 9(b); /© Archivo Iconografio, S.A. 31(t); / © Bettmann 33(t); /© Ted Streshinsky 34(b); /© Andrew Brookes 43.

Printed in the United States of America

1 2 3 4 5 6 7 8 9 09 08 07 06 05